Insufficient Evidence

A perfect murder is impossible. You can have an undetected murder, but that is not perfect.

So. The best you can do is insufficient evidence. They will know you did it, but can't prove it.

That will have to do.

Contents

Insufficient Evidence

<u>In the Beginning</u>

They say there's no such thing as a perfect murder, only an undetected one.

So. Commit and *undetectable* one! That's as close as anyone could hope to come.

Would that take away the reason? It would surely take away Clancy O'Dennis!

Would that be enough?

No. It would take away one of four major targets.

Why O'Dennis first? He's the one I want to wonder and be scared shitless. Forbert first. He's the least of the top four.

Stupid! Life's been wasted taking out the top, directly. That would also be a clue as to what was happening. It's not going to be undetectable if it's obvious!

So! The problem becomes that it will have to be detected for any of it to work. I want to make it plain what is happening. It has to be detected, and right from the first.

Where does that leave me?

Well, if it's detectable, it is a matter of it being ... unsolvable! There are probably a hundred unsolvable murders committed every day!

Why are they unsolvable?

Like this morning's news. The trial against that fat, crooked, disgusting politician. Insufficient evidence to bring the case to trial. Case dismissed, or continued. That's perfect! They can even know who did it, but can't prosecute!

I've lived a wasted life, to this point. Of course, I didn't know enough to see what was happening – then.

"Stuart! You get your stinking snotty ass in here! Right the hell *now*!" Mother [Anne-Marie Kinsey] screeched.

She screeched a lot.

"God! Why have you put this crap on *me*? What have I ever done to deserve this *shit* all the time!

"You get in here and clean this up! Right the hell *now*! You hear me, you little bastard seed? Your father will be home any minute, and he'll take it out on *me*!

"Get in here! Right the hell *now*!"

That's why the mess. I can't do anything, so I'll get Dad to do it for me!

I go into the room, slowly. I know she's going to

hit me, but I also know she better not leave a mark, or Dad really will take it out on her! It would be worth it, if she busted my lip, like she did once before.

Dad pulls the old Ford into the garage, and swears. Good! He's been drinking!

Mom looks scared. I act like I'm trying to get the stuff off the floor [I don't remember what it was, even] and manage to spill something, right in the door. The door opens, and Dad is coming in. He steps in the goo.

"What the hell!!?? Why is this shit on the floor, right where I have to wade through it to get in!? Don't I have enough to do to bust my ass eight hours a day to get a little food here!? You can't even clean a little spot so I can get through without slipping and falling on my ass!?

"What have you been doing all day?! Watching that silly *shit* on TV!? Why isn't my supper ready!? Christ! What I have to go through!"

Yeah, mainly. She did make the bed today, and put some stuff in the washer. It's still there. She never took it out after the wash cycle.

"What?! That shit's been there in the sink since breakfast?! You can't even wash your own dirty dishes?! Bitch! God! I wish I'd never met you! *Bitch*!"

"Oh, Don! I slipped and hurt my ankle, and can't

hardly walk! Stu was trying to help me, but he's only four, so ... Don! Don't hit me! Please!"

Well, she did try to take it away from me, but that was only because she had to come up with some kind of excuse. She didn't hurt her ankle. She laid on the couch and drank half a bottle of MD 20-20 and watched some stupid Fast and Furious movies!

He didn't hit her. Shit! He just dropped the groceries on the table and said he was going to take a shower, and that room better be hospital clean when came back in, or he would strangle her. He wouldn't hit her, he'd choke her 'til she turned blue! He could see the wine bottle on the table. What? He was blind and stupid?

"I'll clean this, Dad. I did spill it."

"Well, she can be glad she didn't do that, at least. Clean it up, and don't let me come home to this crap again, got it? She won't be the only one I choke the shit out of!"

He went into the bedroom. Mom said, "Thanks. I'm sorry I yelled at you. You could have not said anything, and he would take it all out on me! I wish I could get away from him – and you, for that matter. Sometimes I think you're setting me up, then you do something like that. I guess I do drink a *little* more than I should.

"I'll do the dishes. Try to stay away from him

tonight."

I cleaned the stuff up, and went to bed. That worked just about like I planned!

Funny. I can't remember what I'd planned, back then.

Billy and Sheila Dugan! They're way down on the list! They're so superior to everybody, and make mean remarks, then look so innocent you could puke. Brother and sister, but they're always together. The way they pet each other and giggle and like that, you have to know they're a lot more than just brother and sister! Perverts. Catch them together, when they're up to what they almost have to be up to. Two major problems solved! No one would think I had anything to do with it! After all, we don't even speak to each other in the hallway at school!

Okay. It's Tuesday. They'll do the school theater group tomorrow, then go home about five thirty. Their parents will be at the country club on Wednesdays until about 10:30. Plenty of time, and I can figure what they'll be doing, alone in that big house. The maid goes home at seven. That's more than three hours.

If you're going to do a thing, do it. No excuses, no putting it off.

Project Perfect starts tomorrow night at 8:00!

"Bill, we can go to the entertainment room after dinner and practice our lines," Sheila said, for the benefit of the maid, Ethel, who would be leaving as soon as dinner was cleaned up. "My timing's not quite right when I'm supposed to meet Dr. Jekyl. I'm too late, by seconds, to register the look I want. I want to look a little scared and a little, sorta like, 'What's with this creep?' It has to be immediate, or it looks rehearsed."

"Sure, Sis. I have to get the detective bit a little better, too. I can't connect how I'm supposed to figure it from the clues they give me. Maybe Mr. Ames will add one little thing that would connect it. It can come right before the end. It simply isn't there, the way it's written. I'm supposed to figure they're the same person ... but there's no reason I would."

"I've thought of that. I'm only in the play as your secretary ... maybe, if I were to see the Hyde personality in the crowd scene ... because I've already met with Jekyl ... and Hyde is in that scene ... so ... I see him, and they're the same person, which I run to tell you! It would give me a reason to be in the play at all, and would, as we say, fill the dead space!"

"Cool! It's the thing that makes it work! Ames always said the actors have to fill in those dead spaces in any play, and it will make it work, at the same time! Brilliant! You were in the play simply because it is one that doesn't need a knockout type, and you're his top study, so it will ... brilliant!"

"I am leaving now," Ethel announced. "If you will open the gate for me?"

Sheila, clicked the electronic gate lock open. She would close it after Ethel was outside. She and Billy went into the entertainment room. The gate buzzer sounded, so Sheila clicked the security lock on. She grinned at Billy, and they took off their clothes.

"Don't you just love Wednesdays?" Sheila said. "The one night we know we'll have the house to ourselves!

"Did you find a good video?"

"Yeah! PornHub got in a new batch, and I downloaded two really kinky things. One is something we've never even tried! It will be really great!

"I have one that's really massive! Trouble is, we need two guys with it.

"Who could we get to join us in this? I wish we

knew somebody who can have some fun, and who won't ever blabber about it.

"He has to be bi. I don't know anyone like that – that I'm sure about. Maybe Carl Forbes, but I'm not sure he's bi. He may just be gay, and that would only work to a point."

"Have you ever thought about the bi bit?"

"Sure. I might, for something like that."

He plugged a memory stick into the TV, and selected a video. He turned it on, and went to lay on the big sofa. Sheila came to lay on top of him. She watched a minute of the video, and said, "Other than the fact he's hung a lot more than you, I don't see ... oh! Wow! Is that for *real*?!"

"Wait a minute. It gets even better! We *have* to try ... *that!*"

"You got that right! We ... what was that?" There was a sound of something falling in the next room. They listened, but there wasn't anything more.

"Well, we know there's no way anybody got in here, with that security system!" Billy said. "C'mere!" They really got into it, Sheila on top – most of the time.

A few minutes later, a voice said, "An idiot could watch this place for a couple of hours and find ten ways to get in!"

Then, blackness.

"Well, let's see what we've got," Det. Lt. Rod Hardoner [hated that name. Never would forgive his parents.] [Joke. He really got a kick out of it, sometimes] said, sourly. "The Dugans got home about ten thirty, and found them in the den – or whatever you call it – dead. They were in the middle of having some kind of sex orgy, and knocked over a bottle of lime juice. It spilled into a can of ant poison, and a cloud of cyanide gas knocked them off in seconds

"Why was the lime juice ... okay. For the booze they were drinking.

"But why was there sodium cyanide in that particular spot – and open? Was it enough to kill them that fast?"

"Dugan said it was for the fire ants that were by the foundation to the house," Det. Lt. Vicki Dean, his partner, replied. "He said it was there, because they put it in the drawer of the lamp stand. Maybe it was on the lamp stand, and got knocked off when somebody reached for the juice."

"Sound logical to you?"

"No. Stranger things have happened."

"Why would he be trying to shut up evidence of murder?"

"The victims were brother and sister. They were in what is called a 'compromising situation.' The video that was playing was downloads of things on the porn sites. They are in a social level that must not have any such scandals."

"They are? Where they would try to hide that their own kids were murdered?"

"Political connections. He's a campaign manager."

"Why would that ... Republican?"

"Uh-huh."

"Shit!"

"That covers it. We will now be convinced that it was an unfortunate accident that happened – this is from the Mrs. – while they were rehearsing for the school play, next month. The sexual situation will not be mentioned. The videos will not be mentioned.

"She seemed to care a lot more about their 'position' than about her perverted offspring."

"Rod? Vik? We found something. Your Dugan case was murder. There is a video ... here. It's a copy. The original is in CSI lockup," Vinnie Gotti, CSI, said, handing the video to Vicki. "Your killer is probably in the high-income brackets. The camera that was used is *very* high tech."

"How high tech?" Rod asked.

"Better than the ones used in those porn things on the other memory sticks. About two grand better."

"Find the camera, find the killer?" Vicki asked.

"Could damned well be! Ciao!"

Rod took the memory stick, inserted it into their monitor player, and started it. It was from when Billy and Sheila first entered the room. It was clear, and the sound was excellent. It ended just as the sound was heard from the next room.

"So. The only clue we have to prove it was murder is the fact this video exists. It doesn't actually prove it, in the video," Vicki suggested. "They were alive when the video ended."

"This was really well set up," Rod said. "If we find the camera, the one using it can just say that we have several videos from that house, and they're porn videos, which is what they were making, there. The one taking the video left as soon as the video was made, and they were fine. They said they were going to have a drink or two, then go to bed, and they would collect their pay as soon as the video was sold. There were sites that payed *big* for brother – sister vids!"

"Shit!"

"We already agreed on that one!"

"That little Stick-Em note on the memory stick has to be a clue. It sort of scares me. It looks too much like a serial killer clue. A taunt."

"What note?"

"On the memory stick. I just don't see it as a label. The others had labels, and so did that one, but the note was stuck on top of the label for that one."

"I missed it. Which one?"

"The one on the video of them on the couch. It just said 'PVRT 1-2.'"

Rod thought a moment. "So. Maybe we have a religious nut. Perverts one and two. Meaning there will be more. That *is* scarey!"

*

Well! I hope I didn't forget anything. That was a rush! I could have waited for a few more minutes, then really would have a porn video for the sites! I hope they see the connection, but not until the next one.

The watching of the house for one day showed several ways to get in, but it was when the maid left, when they left the security gate unlocked for two to three minutes, that made it a workable plan. Everyone knew the Dugans were at the country club Wednesday nights for the political meetings.

The video cam he used was a sort of iffy point. It cost more than three thousand dollars. Getting that camera was a stroke of luck! It was one that a drug dealer took in payment. It was stolen in another state, and the dealer had stashed it with a lot of other things. Following him had shown where, so grabbing it while the police were questioning the dealer out on the street was perfect! *He* wasn't going to report that a camera he knew was stolen goods, taken in payment for drugs, was stolen from *him*!

Something else. From the Dugan house. Carl Forbes was a sort of lukewarm friend. He was gay, and in the closet. Even if someone connected the Dugans and the rest of the victims, Forbes wouldn't be part, so they must have the wrong one.

And that was an easy one. He knew about Forbes from following him. [It seems he followed a lot of people. He was good at it. They never knew.]

Maybe he would become a detective, after this was over. He could catch people like himself!

That brought on a giggle.

"Hey, wimp! Get me a Coke!" Edgar Bush snarled at me. I was getting a soda for my lunch. I didn't have enough for two.

"I don't have any money, just for my soda with lunch."

"Then get it for me, or I'll kick your wimpy ass from here to the corner and back!"

"No. Go for it!"

I saw Mr. Jacobs, just behind Bush. He wouldn't let those bullies push us smaller kids around. Bush was a year older, and twice my size.

Bush grabbed at me, and Mr. Jacobs grabbed his arm and said, if he ever hit someone smaller than himself, and he saw it, he was going to break an arm for him.

Bush said he was a minor, and Jacobs had attacked him! He was calling the police!

"And I'll tell them he didn't," I said. "I'll say that you called him a goddamned Jew, and shoved at him. Then they'll arrest you."

"I'll get you for this!" Bush yelled. "You just better be ready for it!"

"You better be ready for when I get you!" I

yelled back.

I was 8 years old, Bush was almost ten. Mr. Jacobs said for me to tell him if Bush ever so much as laid one finger on me. He'd break that finger.

Mr Jacobs always stood up for the little guy. He was nice. He bought me a fruit salad for with my lunch.

Bush threatened me and a lot of the other, smaller kids, even in high school. He was a bully, and stupid. They kicked him out of school twice, but he never learned. He wanted to be kicked out, but his father said he would get a job and support himself if he did drop out, so he stayed. He was too stupid to get any kind of job, and nobody but a couple of people just like him liked him.

I swore, even before then, that, someday, I was going to splatter his brains all over the sidewalk.

Carl Forbes saw Earl Janst, gave him the bedroom eye, and went into the Wal*Mart, to walk along the library aisle by the restaurant. Soon Earl came in, and went directly to the restrooms. Carl waited a minute, then went into the restrooms. He talked with Earl for a minute, agreed to meet him at his apartment, and left.

Along the way to the apartment, Earl stopped to get a bottle of wine and some cheese and crackers. He liked the gay scene, but only from his end of the stick.

That suited them both, just fine. Carl only liked it from the other end. This would be only the third time he went to Carl's place, and he had enjoyed both other times. This was the first time he ever bought anything to bring, but Carl was a more classy type than the few others he had any experience with, and really was a nice guy. No strings attached. No demands. No obligations. No silly "love" shit. They were just having a good time. He considered Carl a friend. No more, no less.

The apartment was just around the corner, half a block, on a little spur road that dead-ended by the canal. No one ever went there, so no one would note when Carl had visitors. Probably a good thing for both of them. People were suspicious of Carl, sometimes. He wouldn't go with the type who blabbed. This was a personal thing, and should stay that way.

*

Carl got to the apartment, where he straightened things up a bit. Earl was a great guy, and honest. They would have a romp, enjoy it, and talk awhile. Maybe a second round, maybe not. It depends on if they both want it.

Earl brought wine and cheese! That was a nice

thought, and Carl really appreciated it. They sat around and chatted a bit. Earl liked to have his chest played with, and Carl liked playing with it. Earl really did have a nice body. Not over-muscled, but strong and smooth – and no fat. Carl was totally turned off by fat. He went to a lot of trouble to see that he didn't gain any weight that wasn't pure muscle. It always disgusted him when some out of shape guy with a beer gut would describe the perfect girl for them. Slim, well formed, hair just so, nice boobs, smooth skin, not much makeup ... like a girl like that would give the jerk a second look? Didn't they even have a mirror?

After a snack and some conversation, they went to the bedroom. It was as great as he knew it would be. Earl was a fantastic lover. He had learned that, if he ever wanted a repeat, he would have to give something to the relationship.

He did that!

They laid together for a few minutes, after the sex. They didn't try to talk, just laid there and let the glow fade, slowly and naturally.

Earl took a shower and dressed. He said he had to get to work. He had the five 'til two shift. He hugged Carl goodbye [he wasn't about to kiss another guy] and left. Carl went back inside the apartment to start cleaning up the glasses and dishes.

There was a light knock on the door. Earl must have forgotten something.

It wasn't Earl. He wasn't in the mood for anyone else, after Earl, but he invited the visitor in. There were some crackers and cheese left, and a little more wine.

He went to the kitchen for a new glass. When he came back, no one was there.

He heard a sound from the bedroom. He wasn't interested. He went in, saying, "Not today, thank you!"

Then, blackness.

*

"This seems so ... unreasonable," Vicki declared. "I knew Carl. He was a decent person, and very quiet with the sex thing. It's obvious someone was here, and that bed has definitely been used. We'll get some prints from the glasses ... Shit! They were washed!"

"The knife and butter knife weren't washed. The plate the cheese and crackers were on wasn't washed. The towel rack on the shower wasn't washed, but they only got blurred prints, there. CSI does have a couple of prints. If they're in the database, we'll know whose they are."

"Yeah. Sandra, from CSI, said they'll run them. Whoever left them is definitely not going to be the killer. Maybe he'll give us a clue as to who is."

"Uh-huh. We can hope.

"There was a note."

"Shit! There was?"

"Yeah. On the refrigerator. P-R-V-T three."

"Then we have a serial killer. It's a game. He thinks he can outsmart us. We have to figure who his next victim will be, and we don't have any real connection with these three. They were all three students at Millcrest High School. Dugans, junior and senior. Forbes, senior. That's it. We have to find who hated all ... there's the religious bit. 'Perverts' one, two, and three."

"That's all we have. Forbes was self-sufficient, but lower middle class, since his parents died in that bus crash ... maybe ... but the Dugans didn't have any connection, whatever, to that, and the Dugans were the very rich. The Dugans were snobs, Forbes was gregarious and popular, and never said anything negative about anyone, if his friends can be believed.

"Vik, the only connection is with sex. Maybe they all three turned someone down, in a nasty way?"

"The Dugans would, I think. Forbes would simply say they weren't compatible types, but thanks for the ego boost that they would want him. We don't even have that. We have to wait for the next one. Maybe it will give us something.

"I don't like the idea that we can't do anything until there are more bodies. At all!"

"That makes two of us."

A half hour later, Sandra called to say the prints were from a man called Earl Janst, who worked at Gordy's Carry Out Restaurant.

They got in the squad car to drive to Gordy's. Earl was a pleasant, very attractive man. He was really torn up about Carl. He said he spent a little time with him.

"He was a minor," Vicki warned. "Don't say anything you don't have to. We wouldn't bring any charges, because we know very well that he would instigate ... things, but it could get your name on the sexual offenders' list."

Earl didn't have a clue as to who might want to harm Carl. Carl was a very decent, popular person.

"Yes. A religious nutcase is what we're afraid we have, here," Rod explained.

"Have you ever considered that the type who would do that kind of thing is a latent homo, himself?" Earl asked.

"Oh, yeah! Except that two others were killed by the same person," Vicki replied. "They weren't much into homosexual ... well, possibly bi sex.

"They were into incest."

"Dugans?"

"Yes, but I didn't say that."

"I sort of suspected it. They were a little too cute and cuddly with each other."

"That was between eight and ten, last Wednesday. Please don't take it the wrong way when I have to ask you where you were, and can you prove it," Rod said.

Earl grinned. "Right here. Fifty customers can prove it."

"I already checked it," Vicki said. "He's out of it."

They chatted a few minutes, then went back to the station.

*

That was good practice. He had almost stopped, because Carl had never done anything to him. Quite the reverse.

He couldn't stop. It would mean defeat in what he was doing. It wouldn't register with the top four – yet.

Time for Clancy?

No. He would have to wait, to have time to get scared. Rick Warren. Number two in importance – and that would give a solid basis for the pervert thing, and would tie O'Dennis into it in a way he couldn't mistake, and couldn't hope to explain.

That biker bitch was on his secondary list, and she and he would get together fairly soon. Maybe even tonight. He was ready.

There was a knock on the door. He could see the police car out front.

Did I miss something? Did someone see me I didn't see?

He answered the door.

"Stuart Kinsey?"

"Yes?"

"I'm Rod Hardoner, this is Vicki Dean. We're with the police.

"We're investigating a murder. He was a classmate of yours, and you talked with him a lot at school.

"Do you know anyone who might want to harm or kill him?"

"What are you talking about? Him *who*?"

So they're fishing. I can see if I'm as good an actor as Billy was!

"Carl Forbes was killed ..."

I staggered pretty good there, didn't I? "Carl?" I squeaked.

"Oh! You didn't know? I thought everyone would know about it, by now," Vicki said, sympathetically.

"But ... but ... Carl?"

"Do you know of anyone who threatened him, or

anything?" Rod asked.

"But ... but Carl ... nobody would threaten Carl! Everybody likes him! Nobody cares that he's probably gay. He's always the first to help any of ... oh, God! *Carl*?"

"Any religious types who would consider him evil for being gay?" Rod asked

Good! That ideas planted! Solid!

"No. None of us are very religious. Anything that makes you smile is a sin! That's just crap! Nobody believes that stuff anymore. Some people are gay, some are bi, some are strictly hetero. Big deal! If it's not your thing, just say it's not your thing. Thanks for the offer.

"People who are Jesus nuts don't mix with any of the rest of us. We let them know they aren't welcome. They have two schools run by churches here. Go to one of those.

"I heard it was those Dugan snobs who were murdered. I guess there were a lot of people who wouldn't care, about them. Not Carl. We all like ... liked ... him.

"Oh, hell! I'm crying about him, and I didn't even know him very close. We were just friends at school. Not anything else. I don't think I'd like the gay stuff. He knew it, and never has ... I guess I wish he would've, but I would say no.

"I'm weird! I don't get myself, sometimes!"

"It's an ego boost when someone considers you sexy," Vicki said. "Thanks. We're trying to sort it out."

They left. Back in the house. *I pulled that one off! Perfect!*

Rick Warren

"You better get this straight, you little punk!" Clancy O'Dennis spat. "You don't ever come on this property again, for any reason! Got it?"

I had cut through the corner of the O'Dennis place on my way to school. Clancy was in the little shed with someone. He had his pants down. He saw me, and ran out.

"We come through here all the time! All of us!" I cried.

He slapped me. Hard. It knocked me down. He was a lot bigger than me. I was 13 and he was 15.

"I'll kill you for that!" I promised. He sneered, and said he wasn't the one they would be burying if I ever tried it!

He always made trouble for me, all the way into high school. He got held back in junior high for a year, and in high for a year. He and his good buddy, Rick Warren. I was going to one day kill him, too!

Rick Warren swaggered into the Billiard Palace, and slapped Annette on the ass as he passed. She made a face at him, and gave him the bird. She really wanted him, and he knew it. All these chicks wanted him. He was a great bed partner, and knew it. He heard about some of the things the guys heard them say when they didn't know anyone could hear.

He also knew none of these pussies could hold a candle to his rep! Do the muff diving bit, and a 69, here and there, and the chicks would flock to you!

He liked the way they always pretended to not want that – but they always went for it, after a drink or toke or two. They pretended he forced them to do it, but that was just the old dominance thing. They really wanted the dominance thing. He and Clance had proved that, a thousand times!

Well, a few times, him, but Clance was the one with the real rep. Women couldn't leave either one of them alone!

He told Irene to get him a cold beer, Heineken.

That was proof enough for him! 19, and never a question if he wanted a beer – or even tequila! They thought he was cool for being held back two years in school. He would graduate this year. He couldn't keep that up, being the oldest student. The regular ones all looked up to him. All that stuff about him being a thug was just jealousy.

He guessed he showed his old man who was top dog in the family! Tell him he couldn't have a

Harley? Right!

Well, he couldn't. He couldn't afford one, but he did have a Suzuki.

He wished his old man had stood up to him, just once.

He wished his old man had given a hot damn about him. Just once.

There was Eileen Bates! She was one *hot* number, if there ever was one. She was older – maybe 24 or 25 – and had a great reputation for the dominance thing.

Only, she wanted to be the dominant one, and he wanted to be the top dog.

Maybe tonight would be the time they both learned a thing or two. He could teach her some things, and he knew damned well she could teach him a thing or six! She had sort of said she would like a tumble. She liked big macho muscle studs – and he was as close as they had, around here. That was a challenge he would meet! She was always putting the other guys in town down for being pansies. She could really hurt a guy with that. She got off on doing it.

She came over, and said, "You gonna put out, or run from me, like all these other wimps around here?"

"I could probably take a little while and teach you what a man is really like. You got a place?

Fifty old bags around my place would call the police if I took even one of these girlie-girlies home."

"I got room. Just you – or do you think you'll need help?"

He laughed. "Maybe you and Annette. I haven't laid her, yet. Two should be enough."

She sneered, and said to come along. She would wear him down to a quivering nub and come back to the Palace to see if there was a man in tonight.

They got on their bikes and headed for her house, about half a mile out of town.

They didn't do any of the prelim stuff. They both knew what they were there for. He stripped as soon as they were inside, and grabbed her as she was stepping out of her leathers. She twisted and dropped him, then climbed on top and started gyrating in his lap. He grabbed her breasts and squeezed a bit, then bit a little hard. She grabbed a leather belt and wrapped it around his neck, pulling his head down. She said she heard he was good at oral, and he'd *better* be as good as they said, or he would learn that you don't hold back with a real woman!

He laughed, and said she could use a lesson or two about what a real man wanted. He was big enough, and the frame was there. He strapped her hands to the rails and began to explore her with his tongue. She moaned, and slipped a hand out of the loose band. She grabbed a soft leather whip. Everything went black. The lights went out.

*

"A double lined two forty with the amperage to trip a 100 amp breaker. Positive in the whip, negative in the frame. He was ... touching her with a wet tongue while he was grounded to the frame. Instant sizzler," Vicki said.

"And a sticky note. PERV four and five," Rod replied. "I guess the major charge they were after was a little less than they got. This sort of makes it definite it's someone out to knock off what they think of as perverts. We're looking for a religious fanatic serial killer."

"I think ... maybe not. We'll have to wait and see. It is, but it isn't, in a real sense."

"You don't make any sense."

"Rod, let's go into the background of all the victims. There's got to be something they have in common, other than the sexual things. They all have to trace back to a single person.

"Our one really big problem is Forbes."

"Forbes?"

"He wasn't a bully. I just get the feeling ... I don't know. I have a nagging feeling about this."

"The Dugans weren't bullies. They were snobs, but not to a really offputting degree. You'd like to

Page 29

smack them around to try to put a little sense in their heads, but that's about it."

"Unless you knew about the sex thing, and tried to insert yourself into it?"

"What do you mean?"

"All these are sexual type things. Types of things some call perverted. There isn't any other connection I can see. Somebody tried to get into it with them, and was rejected. Probably, in a nasty way. A belittling way. A cut-down."

"I don't see...?"

"Like, 'with *that* little pencil-stub prick? Get real!' sort of thing."

"I can see ... something, but it isn't ... quite believable. I can see it with the Dugans, but definitely not with Forbes. Warren and Bates? Not even a maybe, with him. Her? She would be like that, in every case, and nobody would go too far off the rails about it.

"We do have to check on the people they were connected with, in a negative way. There may be a common thread. One person who was more sensitive than the others.

"Our big roadblock is Forbes. We have to concentrate on him. He would be the one all the others – so far – would cut down, not the other way around.

"They have his computer and the memory sticks

with it at CSI. Let's see if they found anything."

"Good idea! I'll call Susan. Maybe she's checked that part out."

She called Susan, to find that Bennie Goode, their expert on comps, had gone through the comp. He would send what he found to their comp.

Ten minutes later, a large file marked <u>Forbes, Carl Arthur, #3711946 </u>was downloaded. Rod opened it, to find a two page list of what was on the comp and in the memory sticks and CDs.

"Would it be under email contacts ... How would we know? A picture storage website. Four point two gigs. Maybe a picture ...

"Vik, have you considered blackmail in this? Maybe Forbes was blackmail ... no. He would be the only one dead. He wasn't the type.

"Let's look through his albums. Maybe we can find ... something."

There were pictures, in one album, of men. The pictures were labeled with a name and date, and a "Y," "F," or "N" number.

"Do you think those are all men he slept with?" Vicki asked. "I can't see him as being that promiscuous."

"I think it has to do with the letter. A lot of the 'F' numbers are girls. There are only a few with the other numbers, and all male. Only a few are pictures with both 'F' and 'N.'

"I've seen most of them around.

"Notice that most of them are semi-nude. No full nudity, but he seems to have liked the slender type. Good pecs and lats. None of them fat, by any extension of fact. Most of them are adult, but some are teenagers. The minor bit wouldn't apply to him. He was. It might be a problem with some of the adults.

"The Dugans are in the 'F' category. That may mean 'F' for 'friend' or something. 'Y' is 'yes' and 'N' is 'no.' Maybe it means he would or wouldn't be interested in a repeat? I think the little ' b' or 's' or 'g' after some of them means straight or bi or gay.

"I see a couple in the 'F' part that have the 'N,' too. They're all males, and are the, I guess you would say, overmuscled types. That could be they're okay as friends, but sex is not in the equation. I see that Warren piece of shit is in that category. The Bush jerk is in it. They're both the type he would definitely not like, in that sense."

"Could be. I have to say he had good taste in men! I would like to date a couple of them, like Andy Cartwright, but he's married, and ... oh!"

"Hmm. Maybe we should call on Andy? He's a yes, I see."

"Rod, you call on him. I don't think I could

handle it, if he's gay."

"Earl isn't gay. There's an 's' after his number. There's an 's' after Andy's number. I know two others here, personally. They are not gay, but Rob makes no secret that he likes a romp with a gay person, if they click on other levels. There's a 'b' after his number, so that may mean bisexual. Kenny Dills is gay, and there's a 'g' after his number. There's a 'N' before it, so I don't know ... maybe it ... I don't know.

"I'll go to talk with Andy. He's a mechanic for Hernando's Auto Repair."

Vicki nodded. "I'll see what I can find in the rest of this. I doubt the killer is among the ones he slept with, but you never know. I *do* think he will be among the friends.

"Maybe not. Maybe that's why Forbes was killed."

Rod sighed, and headed for the squad car. He drove the eight blocks to Hernando's to talk with Andy, who was a sort of friend. He said he knew about the picture, and never denied that he would sleep with a close gay friend. His wife didn't consider that as cheating, and he wouldn't question if she had lesbian friends. Carl had been a very clean, considerate, affectionate friend.

"He told me he had a couple of romps with other gay friends, but was worried about AIDS and such, so wouldn't go with them, usually, unless he knew they were as careful as he was. He didn't need any, uh, 'reciprocal' action. He liked for a man to be a man in bed.

"I only went with him twice. He made it plain that he would like for it to be more, but I have to be a little drunk to consider it. If I was too drunk, more than just friendly drunk, he wouldn't go.

"He didn't drink more than a glass of wine, now and then."

"He was a minor."

"I wish you hadn't brought that up. Am I in trouble"

"No. He propositioned you, not the other way around – didn't he?"

"Uh-huh. At a party at Fern Lake. My wife was visiting her mother while she had an operation, and I hadn't had any for a week. He said he wanted to take care of that, because I was exactly the kind of man he went weak-kneed over. It was sort of a joke that ended up a reality.

"It was kind of great! I'll be honest about that!

"He's the only one I did anything like that with since I was about sixteen."

"Do you know of anyone who would want to kill him?"

"No. I just can't believe anyone did."

"Another married man, whose wife wouldn't

understand?"

"No. *He* brought up that he didn't want any problems like that. Ever. If I felt like it would be cheating, we wouldn't. Period.

"See, he said he wanted to borrow me for a night or two, not to take me.

"My dad had some gay friends. Two of them were the ones who did anything with me when I was fifteen and sixteen. Dad said it was okay, so long as they didn't do anything I didn't want. If it was just to get my rocks off, I didn't have to do anything. If they talked me into anything, and I agreed, that was one thing. If they tried to force me into anything, that was anything but okay.

"My cousin, Fred Lange, was my age. His parents were Jesus freaks, and he was going to hell, even if somebody raped him, if he liked it. If any adult even suggested anything, he was to tell the police and the pastor at the church.

"That kind of guilt-trip bullshit makes me sick! He's a drunk, at thirty two, because he always thinks anything bad that happens is because it's his fault. God made a drunk out of him because he screwed a local whore.

"Not a subject I'm good to talk about." He grinned. Rod returned the grin.

"You wouldn't believe the weird things I've seen. I can't help but feel there's something like that behind this case. Another serial killer doing God's work! Amen!"

"Ain't it the truth!"

They chatted a bit more, then Rod went back to the station. Vicki had a list of names. They were "possibles" in the investigation. There were 29 names on the list, and not even a hint of which were more likely than the others.

*

Well, it progresses! I think they really are falling for the religious nut theory!

I was at Hernando's, by the soda machine, when the cop met Andy. He didn't see me, but I'm damned *good* at being in a place where no one notices me. I spent until Mom ran off with that big Rasta being not seen. I spent until Dad got hit by a truck not being seen by him.

I didn't know there were pictures the cops even bothered to check, but I guess they would do that. I'll be in one or two at Carl's, but so will most people around.

So Andy's dad knew he was getting regular blow jobs from his friends. If I had ever even looked like I might like a blow job, I would be like Andy's cousin, and Dad wasn't religious. It was just the way he was raised.

I got a few blow jobs when I was 14 or 15. It

was alright, but I didn't like it too much. I wanted a girl, not a guy. Wanda Stevens was my first. There were only a couple others. I'm not really into sex much. I guess a guy as handsome as Andy gets all the sex he wants ... but he said he only went with Carl twice. He as much as said there wasn't anyone else except his wife.

Tying it all to religion and sex was a great idea! Now, the cops would run around in circles looking for someone else.

Now for Clancy O'Dennis! He would be going to the retreat by the lake Saturday. It might be hard to make it look like religion had anything to do with it. If I can't make that kind of connection – in the cops' minds – the rest of it wouldn't be half as sweet. I want it to be damned plain that the same one is doing it.

The Light of Truth sect had a party there every Saturday. I saw the signs.

... And they use The Copyist place to print out their church notes and such! This could be perfect!

I go to The Copyist with a memory stick. I'm in luck! Miss Robertson is there with several others from the church! I get in line, pay the girl at the cage my $0.20 for a copy page, wait until the guy ahead finishes with the letter-size machine, insert my memory stick, get a page. Very clear. Perfect!

Now for a way to handle it. *This one, I want to be in his face when I rid the world of his sorry ass!*

I watch the nine church people get off their private bus and go to their area. It is a pretty spot, high on the ridge, actually, away from the lake, but a distance from Suicide Cliff, which is on a side branch of the path. There is a drop of about 50 feet to a very sharp grade rocky fall to the canyon, about ninety feet lower. I dropped a rock off the ridge once, and it went all the way to the bottom. It bounced a lot.

They call it Suicide Cliff because two people committed suicide there a few years ago. [That they were never sure was suicide.]

There is a little path, about three feet wide, that runs along, maybe eight or ten feet below the top. It goes to a little cleft, sort of steep, but climbable, to a ditch to the back road. I smirk, and know exactly how I'll handle it. O'Dennis can't resist a challenge from someone he calls a pussy punk, and we wouldn't be in sight of the church people.

I've practiced using the sticks. A lot. I can hit the point exactly, every time.

I make it a point for several people there to see me getting on my trail bicycle and heading back toward town. I put the bicycle near the run-off ditch, behind a bush, and go back to watch from a copse of cedar trees.

About 20 minutes later O'Dennis comes on his bike. A big Honda he's chopped and stretched. He leaves it by the road by the path to the church. He goes to stand under a tree by a picnic table, looking over the people down by the lake.

I go to his bike, grab the pool cue he always carries, and push the bike over. He spins to see me, and I run down the church path. He yells, and comes after me. I manage to be seen by him as I turn down the cliff path. I run down the Suicide Cliff, and to its narrowest part. I step back against the face, to where he won't see me until he's on the path, below where we can be seen from above.

He yells a few profanities, and comes around to where I have the perfect opening to hit him, hard, in the throat, with a one inch piece of aluminum tubing with some lead in one end. He drops to his knees, grabbing at his throat. He can't breathe. I broke the cartoid. I move to stand over him. "I promised you, a long time ago, that I would kill you. Today's the day!

"Remember me? The little pussy wimp? The one you always punched and made remarks about?

"Don't pass out on me, just yet!

"I want you to think, as your last thoughts, just

what kind of slimy piece of shit you are! Welcome to Hell!"

He claws at the dirt. I shove him toward the edge. He goes limp. I push him over the edge, and yell, "No! Not you!" into my cupped hand as he falls. I can hear the church people coming. I throw the aluminum tube as hard as I can out to where it will fall a pretty fair distance from Clancy's body as I go to the cleft and, as fast as I can, up the ditch to my bicycle, and race, as fast as I dare, down Lake Road, toward town. It's steep enough that I make very good time, I practiced that run a lot, a couple of years ago, when I thought I would like to be a bicycle racer. I stop at Lakeview Park and put the half-eaten sandwich and half a Coke on the table, and sit. Less than half a minute later, the police car came by, racing toward the lake. I managed to be seen [I also know how to be seen when I want!] by the police woman in the passenger side. She was the one who came to my house. She had a videocam, and pointed it at me as they went by.

Everyone knew she used the cam when they were chasing someone, so it was a good bet she would be using it to record anyone they passed. No one could come from the lake and not be seen as they came up the road. They weren't moving very fast, because the road curved away from

Lakeview Point pretty sharply, so they had to slow down.

I put the sandwich wrapper and the soda can in the waste basket there, and went on home.

*

"Oh, shit!" Vicki cried.

"What?" Rod replied. She pointed to the note taped to the overturned motorcycle:

PVRT 6

burn in hell with your father in his kingdom spawn of Satan

Vicki took a 9-1-1 call from some woman at a church meet who said a man had jumped, or had been pushed, off of Suicide Cliff. The people at the meeting heard him yelling and swearing something awful, then had heard him yell about someone, and had fallen – or been pushed – off the cliff. His body was a mangled mess, a hundred feet below. They had come up Lake Road, with her using the video camera to record all the cars they passed, going either way [three up and one down] and the two people along the way. A local character who collected aluminum cans, and that student, Kinsey.

"We have to get everyone's story. CSI is on the way, and will check the scene." They had to get those people away. Luckily, only one had gone down the path to the place where he went over. It was a little ledge that was pure rock, so might have some kind of clue about ... something.

Rod shook his head. "I had hoped there would be something that would say it wasn't a religious nutcase. That note makes that a lost cause."

"I don't think so. That isn't a Sticky Note, it's a printed note. It could be a copy killing."

"No. It couldn't. We didn't let out that there were any notes. Either this is the same killer, or we have a copycat working at the station. No one at the station had any opportunity in more than any one of the murders."

"They would have to be CSI. They're the only ones beside us who know about the notes."

"Well, let's talk to some of the people here."

They found Sister Sutcliff, who called 9-1-1. She didn't know anything, except they heard the yelling, then had come to see the body below.

"Did you see anyone, at all, near this area?" Vicki asked.

"No. Just our little crowd. We were all together all the time since we got here."

"Did you see anyone earlier?"

"No. Well, when we got off the bus there were some people on the lake path. The motorcycle wasn't there. We heard it come about five minutes before the yelling."

Rod had an idea. "Did you see anyone on the

lake road when you came up?"

"See anyone? I don't ... maybe someone near Lookout Point, or Lakeview Point. I'm not sure.

"Ask Danny! The bus driver! He would be the one who saw anyone!"

Rod went to find Danny, while Vicki went to the people by the lake. Danny said he saw someone near Lakeview Point. There may have been a bicycle, but he didn't notice it much.

Vicki asked if anyone had seen anyone earlier, before the hubub at Suicide Cliff.

Lanny Drake said the Kinsey boy was there when they came. He had said hello when Stu was getting on his bicycle to head back to town

"How long was that before the Suicide Cliff incident?"

"About twenty or twenty five minutes, I suppose. Not much more than that."

"Did he have anything on the bicycle?"

"What do you mean? He had a plastic sack in the basket, I think ... from Submarine. I remember that. I always thought that was a stupid name for a sandwich shop."

"Did anyone else leave since the fall, before we showed up?"

"The Owens left about two minutes before. They were loading their car when the noise started, and said they didn't care to have to hang around if there were any questions or anything. They just came to fish, then he goes to work at one."

"They were loading the car when the noise, as you call it, started?"

"Yeah."

"Thanks." She went back to talk with Rod. CSI brought the body up. It was that thuggy motorcycle bum, Clancy O'Dennis.

Vicki said, under her breath, that whoever shoved that asshole over a cliff should get a medal. Rod heard her, and grinned.

"He thought he was some kind of super stud. He and Warren were a pair of peas. He was plain disgusting!

"He and Warren were the main school bullies. If it was just them, I'd consider it almost JH. Inevitable, in today's world, that someone would go over the edge that they had tormented for long enough."

Vicki nodded. Sandra came over to report that there was no way to know if he was dead or just dying when he went over. The cartoid was broken, and he died as much from that as from the other dozen fatal blows. It could have been broken when he went through some small trees, or from a rock, or something. Less than 50-50 of showing anything different. "If those people hadn't heard his yell about someone being there, we would put it to accidental, seeing nothing whatever points to anyone else being there.

"I do want to check something out. I want to know if he was on drugs. He might have been hallucinating. Can you picture him dumping that moto, and not picking it up?"

"The note wouldn't be there, in that case," Rod pointed out.

"Oh. There was a note on this one, too?"

"Yes."

"Shit!"

"We're all saying that a lot on this case!" Vicki replied.

*

Perfect! Now I have to make it reasonable that it was me.

What? I'm that stupid? I wanted to take care of those four, and not be detected. I'm there! Right now!

I'll have to take care of Dobbs and Bush. It's not an outsmarting game anymore. That was a stupid idea. All I had to prove was to myself.

So! Which one? They should be easy, but the cops will be watching them. I can't be noted as asking about any of them. That would be a mistake. Don't blow it now.

Dobbs will be at the school gym. He's not as stupid as O'Dennis or Warren, so he might have figured it out – that someone was killing off his kind of asshole bastards. He would never figure it for me. He thinks I wouldn't have the nerve to actually stand up for myself that much.

Well, Surprise! Mr. Dobbs!

I casually stroll past the gym. Dobbs is packing stuff into his truck. His personal stuff.

?

I wonder what the hell that's about. I manage to meet Mrs. Yount, his equal with the girls' sports. She's talking with Harry, the janitor. She said he offered his resignation for personal reasons, and was moving to Brownsville, Texas. He had a job offer there.

So! He did figure it out! Just as good! Just so we're rid of him here!

That leaves Edgar Bush. He's smarter than Dobbs, in some ways, but is a little worse, in others. He's too much like Warren was.

Do I want to kill him to his face?

No. He's just another one of a type the world has too many of, and he directly treated me like shit. I think the others are figuring it out, and know they're about to get knocked off, so they'll think hard about it, particularly now, when it's being shown that bullies result in those mass shootings.

There will be one different problem with him. He's a big deal with that evangelical church bunch.

Maybe that will be a little point in my favor. He's indoctrinated, so is easy to attack, psychologically.

I think, just maybe, I can make it look like he was the one doing all the killing!

I have to think about this. This will be the real challenge!

List things. Bush is a loner, so it might be possible to place him where he could have done all of them.

Check out where he was when each of them were killed. If he was ever anywhere he couldn't have done it, it's back to plan basic.

Yes! Something I heard, a year ago, or more! It would explain it, and Carl will be why it works! Bush is a loudmouthed homophobe, and used to down Carl in a very nasty way, then he suddenly stopped, and said it was unChristian to do that, and he apologized. He got along with Carl after that by just avoiding him.

Carl had said that most homophobes were latent, and were terrified that they were gay. They were attracted to guys, and went to those silly extremes to try to deny it – to themselves!

The police would, very naturally, have checked on where everyone was at the times of the murders. He had gone to a lot of trouble to make it look like he was somewhere else, like with O'Dennis. They might suspect it was *possible* he was there, but very unlikely. If they knew about him practicing racing along that stretch of lake Road, they would be damned suspicious.

They didn't.

So! Find out where Bush was at each of the times the murder could have been committed, and how strong that defense was.

The Dugans, he knew where he was. At home. Alone. He very easily could have done it.

Forbes, he was at the Night Owl Bar. He was also at the Blue Moon, or between them, at the time. It took five minutes. The Blue Moon was only about two blocks from Carl's place. No alibi there!

Warren and Eileen The Bitch, he was, supposedly, visiting friends in Perryville. On his bike. Perryville was at the end of the road to The Bitch's house! No alibi there!

Where was he earlier today?

At the bikers' rally at the college stadium.

Supposedly.

Eddie-boy, you are going DOWN!

I put the memory stick with the subliminal psychological manipulation techniques back into the reference file box, and sat back to think.

Bush was an easily manipulated type. He was insecure, and had an inferiority complex. He used mild drugs, such as marijuana. He drank. He was in a cult type of church. It was doubtful he actually believed any of it, but he didn't consider things. He reacted.

He spent some time in an "uncertain reality" state. The pot, mixed with a beer or two. He would lay in that hammock on the porch at his house. His parents had left the area almost three years ago, and he had stayed. He never got along with his parents. They had him in the cult because it was the only control they had.

He read some of those semi-porn books he downloaded free on the net.

I spent four days and evenings watching his every move. It was easy, because of my talent to not be noticed. I would go a few blocks away when he was dozing to be seen, then was back.

I knew what I was going to do!

I went to Perryville to buy two cheap mobile phones.

Then I waited until he sat by his comp with a beer and had a couple of tokes of pot. He was reading a downloaded book that I had sent to his email. It was, supposedly, a gift in a promotion of a indie authors' offerings. He had downloaded some things from the site. This was a novella called *Darkness, Beautiful Darkness*. It was about a killer who was schizophrenic.

I also sent him two emails from Louise Flanders, a name I made up to sort of flirt with him through emails. I had claimed to have met him at the biker rally. It was just as Traildirters was taking the stage. I had asked why he was leaving. They were a great band! He said he had something he had to do, then he'd be back. It shouldn't take long – but he hadn't come back.

I think that was about the hour when the Dugans were taken out.

There was one from "Louise" just after the book. It asked why he hadn't talked to her when she waved at him at the lake the other day. It was the day that guy jumped off of Suicide Cliff. Just after ... "Oh! Silly me! With all that running around and the cops and all, you didn't even see me! I can be so dense sometimes!"

Ah! He's getting into the book! Now I'll start

talking, real low, through the phone just behind his head under the cushion!

I say things like, "I know what that was like! Same thing happened to me!"

"That's the same type of crud I can be. It's like I'm watching Clance, sometimes. Asshole!"

"That one damned well deserved to die! It was a lot faster than I would have done it!"

"I have to admit, every one of them deserved worse than they got!"

"Oh, shit! I woke up with bruises a couple of times I didn't remember where I got them!"

"Oh, shit! Is this about *me*?! This guy is inside my head on that one!"

"Yeah! I've had people ask me about things they say I did, and I didn't even know who they were or what they were talking about!"

I based the remarks on where I estimated he'd be in the book. It was a little more than two hours later, when he had finished the book, that he laid in the hammock and went to sleep. I got the phone from the chair cushion and left.

Apparently, he was used to hearing very faint voices coming from nowhere.

Now, to wait!

*

Edgar Bush walked into the Handy-Dandy Depot, ordered a couple of breakers for his new connector box, bought an iron skillet [it had been years since he saw one in a store window! His mother always said it was impossible to make proper corn bread in anything but cast iron.] got a few groceries, and headed back home.

He wasn't stupid. Somebody was knocking over the people like he used to be [he still was. He worked hard to control it]. He wondered if he was on their list.

He was very worried about one thing: Carl Forbes. He had as much as raped him, and it messed up his own head, because it was true that he was attracted, and that he responded to it.

It scared pure hell out of him. He didn't want to be gay.

Carl had understood, and said he was to stay away from him, or he'd have to tell about it, in self-defense. He would actually be a good lover if he would simply admit to himself that he could share affection with another man. He said I might be a bit bi, but I wasn't gay, in the faggot sense.

Maybe he deserved getting killed. He didn't really believe in the religious bit. It actually didn't make sense. He didn't believe there was any heaven or hell, but he was scared shitless that there was.

He was an asshole. He had accepted that a long time ago. He treated everybody like shit, and got pissed when they treated him the same way. All somebody was doing now was getting rid of people like him. They probably had damned good reason to.

Who could it be? None of them had the balls to actually stand up to a person ... which is exactly the way of thinking that made him an asshole.

Was *he* actually the killer? Was he insane? A schizophrenic, who killed people, and didn't remember it? He certainly couldn't account for the times they were killed.

He'd asked himself a lot of times the past few days if that was the case. He could see it, with Warren and O'Dennis, and even Eileen, who had cut him down unmercifully.

The Dugans? Was the fact they were so snobby they would drown if they got caught in a rainstorm, and were obviously Satanist ... there he goes! Don't believe it, but claim it against others! Asshole!

There were a lot of holes in his memory since Carl. Had that pushed him over the edge?

He wouldn't hurt Carl again, much less kill him. He wanted Carl to like him, to forgive him. It was the most important thing in his life, and now Carl was dead, and would never like him. He did forgive him. Carl was a lot more of a Christian, in the way he acted, than Ed could ever pretend to be.

Did he kill all of them because they treated Carl ... then he definitely would *not* kill Carl.

He was totally screwed up. It was past time for him to admit it. Maybe he could be helped. Maybe not. He couldn't go on living this way.

There he was! Standing dead in front of the police station! He didn't remember turning that way at Maple Lane!

He sighed, and went in to ask to speak with the officer who was in charge of the recent killings.

What about? Did he have evidence to present?

"I'm not sure. I may have figured out who did them."

"Who? How sure are you?"

"Me, and no, I'm not sure. It's just ... that ... I want to know if I'm crazy, and if I'm killing people!"

"Are you serious!?"

"I'm seriously screwed up. I have to know!"

She took him in to meet the two officers who had asked him about the Dugans.

*

Vicki watched as Rod questioned the Bush character, who was a mental case. She had always seen him as a strange type. Christian bully.

She had known his parents. She could see how he was so twisted. They weren't the evil type, they were just incompetent, and not fit to be parents. They weren't the brightest stars in the galaxy.

He said a girl saw him at the Suicide Cliff case, and didn't remember seeing her, or even being there. She had talked to him at the rally the night the Dugans were murdered, and he didn't remember that. She said he was leaving, and said he'd be back, but he hadn't gone back.

He was drinking, so didn't remember anything clearly about that night at all.

"The same girl? Who?" Rod asked.

"Her name's Louise. We email each other."

Vicki went into the room. She smiled at Bush, and asked Rod if he'd made any progress. Rod knew he was to mention whatever they had been discussing when she came in.

"Just the girl who saw Ed at the rally the night the Dugans were killed, and at the lake when O'Dennis took the dive."

"Really? Does he see her often? It would seem odd that he would see her on those two occasions, if she didn't see him at other times – but then, she was at the rally with him, so that would explain it."

"She wasn't with me," Ed said. "She saw me just when I was leaving. That's when I met her."

"Oh? That's odd. What does she look like?"

"I don't remember."

"And the only other time is when she supposedly saw you at the lake?"

"Yes."

"You weren't at the lake. Someone would definitely have seen you. The only bike there was O'Dennis.

"The real killer is using you. Somehow, he was able to get to you psychologically. You wouldn't have stood up to Warren or O'Dennis. You aren't a killer. It's all fantasy.

"That means the killer wants to punish you. He's using your own admitted instability against you.

"This one's clever, and thinks it's intelligence. It's not even close. He's outsmarted himself. He's left a clue."

"A clue?" Rod asked.

"Louise."

Rod looked puzzled. Ed looked lost.

"I don't...?" from Rod.

"Louise doesn't exist. That she was only on two emails is telling. Smart would be to send several, with just two out of them with anything to do with it.

"Mr. Bush, you have been hypnotized, in a sense. You didn't kill anybody."

"But ... I hope ... I'm screwed up. I didn't really believe it. I was just scared. I would never have hurt Carl again. I know that, and I know I would never ... even hurt him.

"I'm scared ... I did hurt him once. I ... I raped him.

"He didn't hold that against me. He even said I would be a good lover if I would let loose. He said I'm not gay. I'm a little bi, and scared, because I was taught that you were a screaming faggot if you ever even wondered if you would like it.

"I'm so fucked up!"

"You have an identity problem. You strike out at others before they get a chance to strike you. You are easy to hurt, and you react like it doesn't affect you. If Forbes said you'd be a good lover, the real you is being hidden from you, by you.

"I've talked with several people who knew Forbes. They all say the same things. He was affectionate and caring, and would be the last person in the world to put anyone else down. He said you would be a good lover? That means he saw through your facade, that you are also an affectionate person."

"I'm a natural born asshole. I have to admit it."

"No. If you were, the last thing you'd do is admit it.

"We have to know who hates you so much they'd try to do this to you."

Ed "Huh"ed. "Throw a dart at a list of people in this town. Fifty-fifty you'd hit someone who hates me."

"No. We'd just hit someone who would like to see you get your ass kicked, royally," Rod said. "We need to know ... you know something?

"Who puts up with you, maybe avoids you a little, and laughs at you when you treat him the way you treat people?"

"Ah-ha!" Vicki exploded.

Ed thought for a minute, shook his head, and put his hands palm upward with a shrug.

"Would it be someone who reacted to Dugans, Warren, Forbes, and O'Dennis the same way?" Rod asked.

"That would be ... no one. If Carl wasn't in it, I could name a couple."

"So that's why Forbes is in it," Vicki said. "I think our killer also thinks he's a better actor than he is."

"You do? Who?" Rod asked.

"Who was a lukewarm friend who was shocked when he was told Forbes was dead, and who managed to actually cry about it? A little too much, wasn't it? Who was just barely in the area where he might thave shoved O'Dennis off that cliff?"

"The Kinsey boy? But ... we can't hope ... there

simply isn't enough to ... we'll have one hell of an impossible job charging him. There simply isn't enough evidence to even consider it! Any judge would have to throw it out, but no prosecutor would touch it, with what we have. Insufficient evidence for a charge to be filed!"

"I could kill someone who killed Carl," Bush said. "Can I go? You've already said it couldn't be me, and that's what I was here for."

Rod waved, and said they would be in touch if they needed anything. Vicki and Rod were staring at the wall when he walked out.

Ed Bush parked his bike in front of Nuggets of Gold takeout, ordered a medium basket, and went around back to the restroom. He stayed there for about ten minutes, then went back around front, got his order [he had to pay with a $50 bill. He didn't have any smaller], and went home.

*

I am getting antsy about this. I don't know if it worked. Bush went in the police department. I hope it was to confess, but I have to know!

There is a knock at the door. Nobody knows I'm here ... but maybe it's the police. They'll want to know what I know about Bush. I'll just say he is an asshole, and I don't know anything about him, and don't want to know.

I open the door

"*You!!*"

Blackness.

*

"It would seem we spoke out of turn when Bush was in the station," Vicki said, drily. "It's only a half hour since he left, and now Kinsey has a wire twisted around his neck."

Page 61

"I'm half tempted to forget we said anything where he could hear us, with this one," Rod replied. "He lives just six or eight blocks away, so he had time. This took less than a minute."

"We don't have any recourse. We have to go question him. I doubt he'll deny it."

They got in the squad car and drove to the Bush house. Ed was sitting at the picnic table in the yard, eating some chicken nuggets. He asked if they thought of something? Did he have anything they could use against the killer?"

"We have to do our job," Rod said. "I'm sorry, but..."

"Mr. Bush! Did you order that chicken basket after you left our office?"

"This? Sure! It's not good if you don't eat it right away. The salad and fries get soggy after about ten minutes."

"You got it at Nuggets of Gold?"

"Yeah. Why?"

"We'll probably be back in a little while. Will you still be here?"

"All afternoon."

She said for Rod to come on, and they went to the car to drive to Nuggets of Gold. It was two blocks from Kinsey's house.

Did Ed Bush stop there within the last hour?

Yes. He got a basket. Paid with a fifty, so they

had to get it okayed. There were some counterfeit ones around.

"He stayed here while it was prepared?" Vicki asked.

"Sure. He didn't get his change 'til he picked up the order."

"He didn't leave, at any time, for more than three or four minutes?"

"I think he went to the pisser. That would only take a couple of minutes. He was right over there." She pointed to the side table by the rest room. "He was there when we buzzed for him to pick it up." She pointed to the light with the sign that said to pick up order number XXX.

"How long does it take to deliver an order like his?" Rod asked.

"Eleven and a half minutes. We timed it so we could tell people how long they had to wait. We don't cook up a bunch of stuff and have it in a steamer."

They went back to the squad car. "He could have done it, if he ran, but he would probably be huffing when he picked up the order," Vicki said. "I don't think we have anything. It's too close to call."

"Yeah. The DA would laugh us right out of the building," Rod said. "Insufficient evidence."

"Somehow, I'm not sorry. It's late enough to

pick up something for dinner. They really do have good chicken here."

C. D. Moulton's works are available on most major outlets as printed or e-books. CD writes the CD Grimes, PI, mysteries, the Det. Lt. Nick Storie mysteries, the Clint Faraday mysteries, the Flight of the Maita science fiction series, books on orchid culture and many others of many types. Mystery, adventure, intrigue, science fiction, humor, fantasy, paranormal, mild erotica, and factual.